The First Christmas Tree

Henry Van Dyke

© 2023 Culturea Editions
Texte et illustration de couverture : © domaine public
Edition : Culturea (Hérault, 34)
Contact : infos@culturea.fr
Retrouvez notre catalogue sur http://culturea.fr
Imprimé en Allemagne par Books on Demand
Design typographique : Derek Murphy
Layout : Reedsy (https://reedsy.com/)
ISBN : 9791041817986
Dépôt légal : Juin 2023
Tous droits réservés pour tous pays

The First Christmas Tree

Henry Van Dyke

The First Christmas Tree

I

THE CALL OF THE WOODSMAN

THE day before Christmas, in the year of our Lord 722.

Broad snow-meadows glistening white along the banks of the river Moselle; pallid hill-sides blooming with mystic roses where the glow of the setting sun still lingered upon them; an arch of clearest, faintest azure bending overhead; in the center of the aerial landscape of the massive walls of the cloister of Pfalzel, gray to the east, purple to the west; silence over all,—a gentle, eager, conscious stillness, diffused through the air like perfume, as if earth and sky were hushing themselves to hear the voice of the river faintly murmuring down the valley.

In the cloister, too, there was silence at the sunset hour. All day long there had been a strange and joyful stir among the nuns. A breeze of curiosity and excitement had swept along the corridors and through every quiet cell.

The elder sisters,—the provost, the deaconess, the stewardess, the portress with her huge bunch of keys jingling at her girdle,—had been hurrying to and fro, busied with household cares. In the huge kitchen there was a bustle of hospitable preparation. The little bandy-legged dogs that kept the spits turning before the fires had been trotting steadily for many an hour, until their tongues hung out for want of breath. The big black pots swinging from the cranes had bubbled and gurgled and shaken and sent out puffs of appetizing steam.

St. Martha was in her element. It was a field-day for her virtues.

The younger sisters, the pupils of the convent, had forsaken their Latin books and their embroidery-frames, their manuscripts and their miniatures, and fluttered through the halls in little flocks like merry snow-birds, all in black and white, chattering and whispering together. This was no day for tedious task-work, no day for grammar or arithmetic, no day for picking out illuminated letters in red and gold on stiff parchment, or patiently chasing intricate patterns over thick cloth with the slow needle. It was a holiday. A famous visitor had come to the convent.

It was Winfried of England, whose name in the Roman tongue was Boniface, and whom men called the Apostle of Germany. A great preacher; a wonderful scholar; he had written a Latin grammar himself,—think of it,—and he could hardly sleep without a book under his pillow; but, more than all, a great and daring traveller, a venturesome pilgrim, a high-priest of romance.

He had left his home and his fair estate in Wessex; he would not stay in the rich monastery of Nutescelle, even though they had chosen him as the abbot; he had refused a bishopric at the court of King Karl. Nothing would content him but to go out into the wild woods and preach to the heathen.

Up and down through the forests of Hesse and Thuringia, and along the borders of Saxony, he had wandered for years, with a handful of companions, sleeping under the trees, crossing mountains and marshes, now here, now there, never satisfied with ease and comfort, always in love with hardship and danger.

What a man he was! Fair and slight, but straight as a spear and strong as an oaken staff. His face was still young; the smooth skin was bronzed by wing and sun. His gray eyes, clear and kind, flashed like fire when he spoke of his adventures, and of the evil deeds of the false priests with whom he had contended.

What tales he had told that day! Not of miracles wrought by sacred relics; nor of courts and councils and splendid cathedrals; though he knew much of these things, and had been at Rome and received the Pope's blessing. But to-day he had spoken of long journeyings by sea and land; of perils by fire and flood; of wolves and bears and fierce snowstorms and black nights in the lonely forest; of dark altars of heaven gods, and weird, bloody sacrifices, and narrow escapes from wandering savages.

The little novices had gathered around him, and their faces had grown pale and their eyes bright as they listened with parted lips, entranced in admiration, twining their arms about one another's shoulders and holding closely together, half in fear, half in delight. The older nuns had turned from their tasks and paused, in passing by, to hear the pilgrim's story. Too well they knew the truth of what he spoke. Many a one among them had seen the smoke rising from the ruins of her father's roof. Many a one had a brother far away in the wild country to whom her heart went out night and day, wondering if he were still among the living.

But now the excitements of that wonderful day were over; the hours of the evening meal had come; the inmates of the cloister were assembled in the refectory.

On the dais sat the stately Abbess Addula, daughter of King Dagobert, looking a princess indeed, in her violet tunic, with the hood and cuffs of her long white robe trimmed with fur, and a snowy veil resting like a crown on her snowy hair. At her right hand was the honoured guest, and at her left hand her grandson, the young Prince Gregor, a big, manly boy, just returned from school.

The long, shadowy hall, with its dark-brown raters and beams; the double rows of nuns, with their pure veils and fair faces; the ruddy flow of the slanting sunbeams striking upwards through the tops of the windows and painting a pink glow high up on the walls,—it was all as beautiful as a picture, and as silent. For this was the rule of the cloister, that at the table all should sit in stillness for a little while, and then one should read aloud, while the rest listened.

"It is the turn of my grandson to read to-day," said the abbess to Winfried; "we shall see how much he has learned in the school. Read, Gregor; the place in the book is marked."

The tall lad rose from his seat and turned the pages of the manuscript. It was a copy of Jerome's version of the Scriptures in Latin, and the marked place was in the letter of St. Paul to the Ephesians,—the passage where he describes the preparation of the Christian as the arming of a warrior for glorious battle. The young voice rang out clearly, rolling the sonorous words, without slip or stumbling, to the end of the chapter.

Winfried listened, smiling. "My son," said he, as the reader paused, "that was bravely read. Understandest thou what thou readest?"

"Surely, father," answered the boy; "it was taught me by the masters at Treves; and we have read this epistle clear through, from beginning to end, so that I almost know it by heart."

Then he began again to repeat the passage, turning away from the page as if to show his skill.

But Winfried stopped him with a friendly lifting of the hand.

"No so, my son; that was not my meaning. When we pray, we speak to God; when we read, it is God who speaks to us. I ask whether thou hast heard what He has said to thee, in thine own words, in the common speech. Come, give us again the message of the warrior and his armour and his battle, in the mother-tongue, so that all can understand it."

The boy hesitated, blushed, stammered; then he came around to Winfried's seat, bringing the book. "Take the book, my father," he cried, "and read it for me. I cannot see the meaning plain, though I love the sound of the words. Religion I know, and the doctrines of our faith, and the life of priests and nuns in the cloister, for which my grandmother designs me, though it likes me little. And fighting I know, and the life of warriors and heroes, for I have read of it in Virgil and the ancients, and heard a bit from the soldiers at Treves; and I would fain taste more of it, for it likes me much. But how the two lives fit together, or what need there is of armour for a clerk in holy orders, I can never see. Tell me the meaning, for if there is a man in all the world that knows it, I am sure it is none other than thou."

So Winfried took the book and closed it, clasping the boy's hand with his own.

"Let us first dismiss the others to their vespers," said he, "lest they should be weary."

A sign from the abbess; a chanted benediction; a murmuring of sweet voices and a soft rustling of many feet over the rushes on the floor; the gentle tide of noise flowed out through the doors and ebbed away down the corridors; the three at the head of the table were left alone in the darkening room.

Then Winfried began to translate the parable of the soldier into the realities of life.

At every turn he knew how to flash a new light into the picture out of his own experience. He spoke of the combat with self, and of the wrestling with dark spirits in solitude. He spoke of the demons that men had worshipped for centuries in the wilderness, and whose malice they invoked against the stranger who ventured into the gloomy forest. Gods, they called them, and told strange tales of their dwelling among the impenetrable branches of the oldest trees and in the caverns of the shaggy hills; of their riding on the wind-horses and hurling spears of lightning against their foes. Gods they were not, but foul spirits of the air, rulers of the darkness. Was there not glory and honour in fighting with them, in daring their anger under the shield of faith, in putting them to flight with the sword of truth? What better adventure could a brave man ask than to go forth against them, and wrestle with them, and conquer them?

"Look you, my friends," said Winfried, "how sweet and peaceful is this convent to-night, on the eve of the nativity of the Prince of Peace! It is a garden full of flowers in the heart of winter; a nest among the branches of a great tree shaken by the winds; a still haven on the edge of a tempestuous sea. And this is what religion means for those who are chosen and called to quietude and prayer and meditation.

"But out yonder in the wide forest, who knows what storms are raving to-night in the hearts of men, though all the woods are still? who knows what haunts of wrath and cruelty and fear are closed to-night against the advent of the Prince of Peace? And shall I tell you what religion means to those who are called and chosen to dare and to fight, and to conquer the world for Christ? It means to launch out into the deep. It means to go against the strongholds of the adversary. It means to struggle to win an entrance for their Master everywhere. What helmet is strong enough for this strife save the helmet of salvation? What breastplate can guard a man against these fiery darts but the breastplate of righteousness? What shoes can stand the wear of these journeys but the preparation of the gospel of peace?"

"Shoes?" he cried again, and laughed as if a sudden thought had struck him. He thrust out his foot, covered with a heavy cowhide boot, laced high about his leg with thongs of skin.

"See here,—how a fighting man of the cross is shod! I have seen the boots of the Bishop of Tours,—white kid, broidered with silk; a day in the bogs would tear them to shreds. I have seen the sandals that the monks use on the highroads,—yes, and worn them; ten pair of them have I worn out and thrown away in a single journey. Now I shoe my feet with the toughest hides, hard as iron; no rock can cut them, no branches can tear them. Yet more than one pair of these have I outworn, and many more shall I outwear ere my journeys are ended. And I think, if God is gracious to me, that I shall die wearing them. Better so than in a soft bed with silken coverings. The boots of a warrior, a hunter, a woodsman,—these are my preparation of the gospel of peace."

"Come, Gregor," he said, laying his brown hand on the youth's shoulder, "come, wear the forester's boots with me. This is the life to which we are called. Be strong in the Lord, a hunter of the demons, a subduer of the wilderness, a woodsman of the faith. Come!"

The boy's eyes sparkled. He turned to his grandmother. She shook her head vigorously.

"Nay, father," she said, "draw not the lad away from my side with these wild words. I need him to help me with my labours, to cheer my old age."

"Do you need him more than the Master does?" asked Winfried; "and will you take the wood that is fit for a bow to make a distaff?"

"But I fear for the child. Thy life is too hard for him. He will perish with hunger in the woods."

"Once," said Winfried, smiling, "we were camped by the bank of the river Ohru. The table was spread for the morning meal, but my comrades cried that it was empty; the provisions were exhausted; we must go without breakfast, and perhaps starve before we could escape from the wilderness. While they complained, a fish-hawk flew up from the river with flapping wings, and let fall a great pike in the midst of the camp. There was food enough and to spare.

Never have I seen the righteous forsaken, nor his seed begging bread."

"But the fierce pagans of the forest," cried the abbess,—"they may pierce the boy with their arrows, or dash out his brains with their axes. He is but a child, too young for the dangers of strife."

"A child in years," replied Winfried, "but a man in spirit. And if the hero must fall early in the battle, he wears the brighter crown, not a leaf withered, not a flower fallen."

The aged princess trembled a little. She drew Gregor close to her side, and laid her hand gently on his brown hair.

"I am not sure that he wants to leave me yet. Besides, there is no horse in the stable to give him, now, and he cannot go as befits the grandson of a king."

Gregor looked straight into her eyes.

"Grandmother," said he, "dear grandmother, if thou wilt not give me a horse to ride with this man of God, I will go with him afoot."

II

THE TRAIL THROUGH THE FOREST

TWO years had passed, to a day, almost to an hour, since that Christmas eve in the cloister of Pfalzel. A little company of pilgrims, less than a score a men, were creeping slowly northward through the wide forest that rolled over the hills of central Germany.

At the head of the band marched Winfried, clad in a tunic of fur, with his long black robe girt high about his waist, so that it might not hinder his stride. His hunter's boots were crusted with snow. Drops of ice sparkled like jewels along the thongs that bound his legs. There was no other ornament to his dress except the bishop's cross hanging on his breast, and the broad silver clasp that fastened his cloak about his neck. He carried a strong, tall staff in his hand, fashioned at the top into the form of a cross.

Close beside him, keeping step like a familiar comrade, was the young Prince

Gregor. Long marches through the wilderness had stretched his limbs and broadened his back, and made a man of him in stature as well as in spirit. His jacket and cap were of wolfskin, and on his shoulder he carried an axe, with broad, shining blade. He was a mighty woodsman now, and could make a spray of chips fly around him as he hewed his way through the trunk of spruce-tree.

Behind these leaders followed a pair of teamsters, guiding a rude sledge, loaded with food and the equipage of the camp, and drawn by two big, shaggy horses, blowing thick clouds of steam from their frosty nostrils. Tiny icicles hung from the hairs on their lips. Their flanks were smoking. They sank above the fetlocks at every step in the soft snow.

Last of all came the rear guard, armed with bows and javelins. It was no child's play, in those days, to cross Europe afoot.

The weird woodland, sombre and illimitable, covered hill and vale, tableland and mountain-peak. There were wide moors where the wolves hunted in packs as if the devil drove them, and tangled thickets where the lynx and the boar made their lairs. Fierce bears lurked among the rocky passes, and had not yet learned to fear the face of man. The gloomy recesses of the forest gave shelter to inhabitants who were still more cruel and dangerous than beasts of prey,— outlaws and sturdy robbers and mad were-wolves and bands of wandering pillagers.

The pilgrim who would pass from the mouth of the Tiber to the mouth of the Rhine must travel with a little army of retainers, or else trust in God and keep his arrows loose in the quiver.

The travellers were surrounded by an ocean of trees, so vast, so full of endless billows, that it seemed to be pressing on every side to overwhelm them. Gnarled oaks, with branches twisted and knotted as if in rage, rose in groves like tidal waves. Smooth forests of beech-trees, round and gray, swept over the knolls and slopes of land in a mighty ground-swell. But most of all, the multitude of pines and firs, innumerable and monotonous, with straight, stark trunks, and branches woven together in an unbroken Hood of darkest green, crowded through the valleys and over the hills, rising on the highest ridges into ragged crests, like the foaming edge of breakers.

Through this sea of shadows ran a narrow stream of shining whiteness,—an ancient Roman road, covered with snow. It was as if some great ship had ploughed through the green ocean long ago, and left behind it a thick, smooth wake of foam. Along this open track the travellers held their way,—heavily, for the drifts were deep; warily, for the hard winter had driven many packs of wolves down from the moors.

The steps of the pilgrims were noiseless; but the sledges creaked over the dry snow, and the panting of the horses throbbed through the still, cold air. The pale-blue shadows on the western side of the road grew longer. The sun, declining through its shallow arch, dropped behind the tree-tops. Darkness followed swiftly, as if it had been a bird of prey waiting for this sign to swoop down upon the world.

"Father," said Gregor to the leader, "surely this day's march is done. It is time to rest, and eat, and sleep. If we press onward now, we cannot see our steps; and will not that be against the word of the psalmist David, who bids us not to put confidence in the legs of a man?"

Winfried laughed. "Nay, my son Gregor," said he, "thou hast tripped, even now, upon thy text. For David said only, 'I take no pleasure in the legs of a man.' And so say I, for I am not minded to spare thy legs or mine, until we come farther on our way, and do what must be done this night. Draw the belt tighter, my son, and hew me out this tree that is fallen across the road, for our campground is not here."

The youth obeyed; two of the foresters sprang to help him; and while the soft fir-wood yielded to the stroke of the axes, and the snow flew from the bending branches, Winfried turned and spoke to his followers in a cheerful voice, that refreshed them like wine.

"Courage, brothers, and forward yet a little! The moon will light us presently, and the path is plain. Well know I that the journey is weary; and my own heart wearies also for the home in England, where those I love are keeping feast this Christmas eve. But we have work to do before we feast to-night. For this is the Yuletide, and the heathen people of the forest have gathered at the thunder-oak of Geismar to worship their god, Thor. Strange things will be seen there, and deeds which make the soul black. But we are sent to lighten their darkness; and we will teach our kinsmen to keep a Christmas with us such as the woodland has never known. Forward, then, and let us stiffen up our feeble knees!"

A murmur of assent came from the men. Even the horses seemed to take fresh heart. They flattened their backs to draw the heavy loads, and blew the frost from their nostrils as they pushed ahead.

The night grew broader and less oppressive. A gate of brightness was opened secretly somewhere in the sky; higher and higher swelled the clear moon-flood, until it poured over the eastern wall of forest into the road. A drove of wolves howled faintly in the distance, but they were receding, and the sound soon died away. The stars sparkled merrily through the stringent air; the small, round moon shone like silver; little breaths of the dreaming wind wandered whispering across the pointed fir-tops, as the pilgrims toiled bravely onward, following their clue of light through a labyrinth of darkness.

After a while the road began to open out a little. There were spaces of meadow-land, fringed with alders, behind which a boisterous river ran, clashing through spears of ice.

Rude houses of hewn logs appeared in the openings, each one casting a patch of inky blackness upon the snow. Then the travellers passed a larger group of dwellings, all silent and unlighted; and beyond, they saw a great house, with many outbuildings and enclosed courtyards, from which the hounds bayed furiously, and a noise of stamping horses came from the stalls. But there was no other sound of life. The fields around lay bare to the moon. They saw no man, except that once, on a path that skirted the farther edge of a meadow, three dark figures passed by, running very swiftly.

Then the road plunged again into a dense thicket, traversed it, and climbing to the left, emerged suddenly upon a glade, round and level except at the northern side, where a swelling hillock was crowned with a huge oak-tree. It towered above the heath, a giant with contorted arms, beckoning to the host of lesser trees. "Here," cried Winfried, as his eyes flashed and his hand lifted his heavy staff, "here is the Thunder-oak; and here the cross of Christ shall break the hammer of the false god Thor."

III

THE SHADOW OF THE THUNDER-OAK

WITHERED leaves still clung to the branches of the oak: torn and faded banners of the departed summer. The bright crimson of autumn had long since disappeared, bleached away by the storms and the cold. But to-night these tattered remnants of glory were red again: ancient bloodstains against the dark-blue sky. For an immense fire had been kindled in front of the tree. Tongues of ruddy flame, fountains of ruby sparks, ascended through the spreading limbs and flung a fierce illumination upward and around. ward and around. The pale, pure moonlight that bathed the surrounding forests was quenched and eclipsed here. Not a beam of it sifted down-ward through the branches of the oak. It stood like a pillar of cloud between the still light of heaven and the crackling, flashing fire of earth.

But the fire itself was invisible to Winfried and his companions. A great throng of people were gathered around it in a half-circle, their backs to the open glade, their faces towards the oak. Seen against that glowing background, it was but the silhouette of a crowd, vague, black, formless, mysterious.

The travellers paused for a moment at the edge of the thicket, and took counsel together.

"It is the assembly of the tribe," said one of the foresters, "the great night of the council. I heard of it three days ago, as we passed through one of the villages. All who swear by the old gods have been summoned. They will sacrifice a steed to the god of war, and drink blood, and eat horse-flesh to make them strong. It will be at the peril of our lives if we approach them. At least we must hide the cross, if we would escape death."

"Hide me no cross," cried Winfried, lifting his staff, "for I have come to show it, and to make these blind folk see its power. There is more to be done here to-night than the slaying of a steed, and a greater evil to be stayed than the shameful eating of meat sacrificed to idols. I have seen it in a dream. Here the cross must stand and be our rede."

At his command the sledge was left in the border of the wood, with two of the men to guard it, and the rest of the company moved forward across the open ground. They approached unnoticed, for all the multitude were looking intently towards the fire at the foot of the oak.

Then Winfried's voice rang out, "Hail, ye sons of the forest! A stranger claims the warmth of your fire in the winter night."

Swiftly, and as with a single motion, a thousand eyes were bent upon the speaker. The semicircle opened silently in the middle; Winfried entered with his followers; it closed again behind them.

Then, as they looked round the curving ranks, they saw that the hue of the assemblage was not black, but white,—dazzling, radiant, solemn. White, the robes of the women clustered together at the points of the wide crescent; white, the glittering byrnies of the warriors standing in close ranks; white, the fur mantles of the aged men who held the central place in the circle; white, with the shimmer of silver ornaments and the purity of lamb's-wool, the raiment of a little group of children who stood close by the fire; white, with awe and fear, the faces of all who looked at them; and over all the flickering, dancing radiance of the flames played and glimmered like a faint, vanishing tinge of blood on snow.

The only figure untouched by the glow was the old priest, Hunrad, with his long, spectral robe, flowing hair and beard, and dead-pale face, who stood with his back to the fire and advanced slowly to meet the strangers.

"Who are you? Whence come you, and what seek you here?" His voice was heavy and toneless as a muffled bell.

"You kinsman am I, of the German brotherhood," answered Winfried, "and from England, beyond the sea, have I come to bring you a greeting from that land, and a message from the All-Father, whose servant I am."

"Welcome, then," said Hunrad, "welcome, kinsman, and be silent; for what passes here is too high to wait, and must be done before the moon crosses the middle heaven, unless, indeed, thou hast some sign or token from the gods. Canst thou work miracles?"

The question came sharply, as if a sudden gleam of hope had flashed through the tangle of the old priest's mind. But Winfried's voice sank lower and a cloud of disappointment passed over his face as he replied: "Nay, miracles have I never wrought, though I have heard of many; but the All-Father has given no power to my hands save such as belongs to common man."

"Stand still, then, thou common man," said Hunrad, scornfully, "and behold what the gods have called us hither to do. This night is the death-night of the sun-god, Baldur the Beautiful, beloved of gods and men. This night is the hour of darkness and the power of winter, of sacrifice and mighty fear. This night the great Thor, the god of thunder and war, to whom this oak is sacred, is grieved for the death of Baldur, and angry with this people because they have forsaken his worship. Long is it since an offering has been laid upon his altar, long since the roots of his holy tree have been fed with blood. Therefore its leaves have withered before the time, and its boughs are heavy with death. Therefore the Slavs and the Wends have beaten us in battle. Therefore the harvests have failed, and the wolf-hordes have ravaged the folds, and the strength has departed from the bow, and the wood of the spear has broken, and the wild boar has slain the huntsman. Therefore the plague has fallen on our dwellings, and the dead are more than the living in all our villages. Answer me, ye people, are not these things true?"

A hoarse sound of approval ran through the circle. A chant, in which the voices of the men and women blended, like the shrill wind in the pine-trees above the rumbling thunder of a waterfall, rose and fell in rude cadences.

O Thor, the Thunderer,

Mighty and merciless,

Spare us from smiting!

Heave not thy hammer,

Angry, against us;

Plague not thy people.

Take from our treasure

Richest of ransom.

Silver we send thee,

Jewels and javelins,

Goodliest garments,

All our possessions,

Priceless, we proffer.

Sheep will we slaughter,

Steeds will we sacrifice;

Bright blood shall bathe thee,

O tree of Thunder,

Life-floods shall lave thee,

Strong wood of wonder.

Mighty, have mercy,

Smite us no more,

Spare us and save us,

Spare us, Thor! Thor!

With two great shouts the song ended, and a stillness followed so intense that the crackling of the fire was heard distinctly. The old priest stood silent for a moment. His shaggy brows swept down over his eyes like ashes quenching flame. Then he lifted his face and spoke.

"None of these things will please the god. More costly is the offering that shall cleanse your sin, more precious the crimson dew that shall send new life into this holy tree of blood. Thor claims your dearest and your noblest gift."

Hunrad moved nearer to the handful of children who stood watching the red mines in the fire and the swarms of spark-serpents darting upward. They had heeded none of the priest's words, and did not notice now that he approached them, so eager were they to see which fiery snake would go highest among the oak branches. Foremost among them, and most intent on the pretty game, was a boy like a sunbeam, slender and quick, with blithe brown eyes and laughing lips. The priest's hand was laid upon his shoulder. The boy turned and looked up in his face.

"Here," said the old man, with his voice vibrating as when a thick rope is strained by a ship swinging from her moorings, "here is the chosen one, the eldest son of the Chief, the darling of the people. Hearken, Bernhard, wilt thou go to Valhalla, where the heroes dwell with the gods, to bear a message to Thor?"

The boy answered, swift and clear:

"Yes, priest, I will go if my father bids me. Is it far away? Shall I run quickly? Must I take my bow and arrows for the wolves?"

The boy's father, the Chieftain Gundhar, standing among his bearded warriors, drew his breath deep, and leaned so heavily on the handle of his spear that the wood cracked. And his wife, Irma, bending forward from the ranks of women, pushed the golden hair from her forehead with one hand. The other dragged at the silver chain about her neck until the rough links pierced her flesh, and the red drops fell unheeded on the snow of her breast.

A sigh passed through the crowd, like the murmur of the forest before the storm breaks. Yet no one spoke save Hunrad:

"Yes, my Prince, both bow and spear shalt thou have, for the way is long, and thou art a brave huntsman. But in darkness thou must journey for a little space, and with eyes blindfolded. Fearest thou?"

"Naught fear I," said the boy, "neither darkness, nor the great bear, nor the were-wolf. For I am Gundhar's son, and the defender of my folk."

Then the priest led the child in his raiment of lamb's-wool to a broad stone in front of the fire. He gave him his little bow tipped with silver, and his spear with shining head of steel. He bound the child's eyes with a white cloth, and bade him kneel beside the stone with his face to the east. Unconsciously the wide arc of spectators drew inward toward the centre, as the ends of the bow draw together when the cord is stretched. Winfried moved noiselessly until he stood close behind the priest.

The old man stooped to lift a black hammer of stone from the ground,—the sacred hammer of the god Thor. Summoning all the strength of his withered arms, he swung it high in the air. It poised for an instant above the child's fair head—then turned to fall.

One keen cry shrilled out from where the women stood: "Me! take me! not Bernhard!"

The flight of the mother towards her child was swift as the falcon's swoop. But swifter still was the hand of the deliverer.

Winfried's heavy staff thrust mightily against the hammer's handle as it fell. Sideways it glanced from the old man's grasp, and the black stone, striking on the altar's edge, split in twain. A shout of awe and joy rolled along the living circle. The branches of the oak shivered. The flames leaped higher. As the shout died away the people saw the lady Irma, with her arms clasped round her child, and above them, on the altar-stone, Winfried, his face shining like the face of an angel.

IV

THE FELLING OF THE TREE

A SWIFT mountain-flood rolling down its channel; a huge rock tumbling from the hill-side and falling in mid-stream; the baffled waters broken and confused, pausing in their flow, dash high against the rock, foaming and murmuring, with divided impulse, uncertain whether to turn to the right or the left.

Even so Winfried's bold deed fell into the midst of the thoughts and passions of the council. They were at a standstill. Anger and wonder, reverence and joy and confusion surged through the crowd. They knew not which way to move: to resent the intrusion of the stranger as an insult to their gods, or to welcome him as the rescuer of their darling prince.

The old priest crouched by the altar, silent. Conflicting counsels troubled the air. Let the sacrifice go forward; the gods must be appeased. Nay, the boy must not die; bring the chieftain's best horse and slay it in his stead; it will be enough; the holy tree loves the blood of horses. Not so, there is a better counsel yet; seize the stranger whom the gods have led hither as a victim and make his life pay the forfeit of his daring.

The withered leaves on the oak rustled and whispered overhead. The fire flared and sank again. The angry voices clashed against each other and fell like opposing waves. Then the chieftain Gundhar struck the earth with his spear and gave his decision.

"All have spoken, but none are agreed. There is no voice of the council. Keep silence now, and let the stranger speak. His words shall give us judgment, whether he is to live or to die."

Winfried lifted himself high upon the altar, drew a roll of parchment from his bosom, and began to read.

"A letter from the great Bishop of Rome, who sits on a golden throne, to the people of the forest, Hessians and Thuringians, Franks and Saxons. In nomine Domini, sanctae et individuae trinitatis, amen!"

A murmur of awe ran through the crowd. "It is the sacred tongue of the

Romans: the tongue that is heard and understood by the wise men of every land. There is magic in it. Listen!"

Winfried went on to read the letter, translating it into the speech of the people.

"'We have sent unto you our Brother Boniface, and appointed him your bishop, that he may teach you the only true faith, and baptize you, and lead you back from the ways of error to the path of salvation. Hearken to him in all things like a father. Bow your hearts to his teaching. He comes not for earthly gain, but for the gain of your souls. Depart from evil works. Worship not the false gods, for they are devils. Offer no more bloody sacrifices, nor eat the flesh of horses, but do as our Brother Boniface commands you. Build a house for him that he may dwell among you, and a church where you may offer your prayers to the only living God, the Almighty King of Heaven.'"

It was a splendid message: proud, strong, peaceful, loving. The dignity of the words imposed mightily upon the hearts of the people. They were quieted as men who have listened to a lofty strain of music.

"Tell us, then," said Gundhar, "what is the word that thou bringest to us from the Almighty. What is thy counsel for the tribes of the woodland on this night of sacrifice?"

"This is the word, and this is the counsel," answered Winfried. "Not a drop of blood shall fall to-night, save that which pity has drawn from the breast of your princess, in love for her child. Not a life shall be blotted out in the darkness tonight; but the great shadow of the tree which hides you from the light of heaven shall be swept away. For this is the birth-night of the white Christ, son of the All-Father, and Saviour of mankind. Fairer is He than Baldur the Beautiful, greater than Odin the Wise, kinder than Freya the Good. Since He has come to earth the bloody sacrifices must cease. The dark Thor, on whom you vainly call, is dead. Deep in the shades of Niffelheim he is lost forever. His power in the world is broken. Will you serve a helpless god? See, my brothers, you call this tree his oak. Does he dwell here? Does he protect it?"

A troubled voice of assent rose from the throng. The people stirred uneasily. Women covered their eyes. Hunrad lifted his head and muttered hoarsely, "Thor! take vengeance! Thor!"

Winfried beckoned to Gregor. "Bring the axes, thine and one for me. Now, young woodsman, show thy craft! The king-tree of the forest must fall, and swiftly, or all is lost!"

The two men took their places facing each other, one on each side of the oak. Their cloaks were flung aside, their heads bare. Carefully they felt the ground with their feet, seeking a firm grip of the earth. Firmly they grasped the axe-helves and swung the shining blades.

"Tree-god!" cried Winfried, "art thou angry? Thus we smite thee!"

"Tree-god!" answered Gregor, "art thou mighty? Thus we fight thee!"

Clang! clang! the alternate strokes beat time upon the hard, ringing wood. The axe-heads glittered in their rhythmic flight, like fierce eagles circling about their quarry.

The broad flakes of wood flew from the deepening gashes in the sides of the oak. The huge trunk quivered. There was a shuddering in the branches. Then the great wonder of Winfried's life came to pass.

Out of the stillness of the winter night, a mighty rushing noise sounded overhead.

Was it the ancient gods on their white battle-steeds, with their black hounds of wrath and their arrows of lightning, sweeping through the air to destroy their foes?

A strong, whirling wind passed over the tree-tops. It gripped the oak by its branches and tore it from its roots. Backward it fell, like a ruined tower, groaning and crashing as it split asunder in four great pieces.

Winfried let his axe drop, and bowed his head for a moment in the presence of almighty power.

Then he turned to the people, "Here is the timber," he cried, "already felled and split for your new building. On this spot shall rise a chapel to the true God and his servant St. Peter.

"And here," said he, as his eyes fell on a young fir-tree, standing straight and green, with its top pointing towards the stars, amid the divided ruins of the fallen oak, "here is the living tree, with no stain of blood upon it, that shall be the sign of your new worship. See how it points to the sky. Let us call it the tree of the Christ-child. Take it up and carry it to the chieftain's hall. You shall go no more into the shadows of the forest to keep your feasts with secret rites of shame. You shall keep them at home, with laughter and song and rites of love. The thunder-oak has fallen, and I think the day is coming when there shall not be a home in all Germany where the children are not gathered around the green fir-tree to rejoice in the birth-night of Christ."

So they took the little fir from its place, and carried it in joyous procession to the edge of the glade, and laid it on the sledge. The horses tossed their heads and drew their load bravely, as if the new burden had made it lighter.

When they came to the house of Gundhar, he bade them throw open the doors of the hall and set the tree in the midst of it. They kindled lights among the branches until it seemed to be tangled full of fire-flies. The children encircled it, wondering, and the sweet odour of the balsam filled the house.

Then Winfried stood beside the chair of Gundhar, on the dais at the end of the hall, and told the story of Bethlehem; of the babe in the manger, of the shepherds on the hills, of the host of angels and their midnight song. All the people listened, charmed into stillness.

But the boy Bernhard, on Irma's knee, folded by her soft arm, grew restless as the story lengthened, and began to prattle softly at his mother's ear.

"Mother," whispered the child, "why did you cry out so loud, when the priest was going to send me to Valhalla?"

"Oh, hush, my child," answered the mother, and pressed him closer to her side.

"Mother," whispered the boy again, laying his finger on the stains upon her breast, "see, your dress is red! What are these stains? Did some one hurt you?"

The mother closed his mouth with a kiss. "Dear, be still, and listen!"

The boy obeyed. His eyes were heavy with sleep. But he heard the last words of Winfried as he spoke of the angelic messengers, flying over the hills of Judea and singing as they flew. The child wondered and dreamed and listened. Suddenly his face grew bright. He put his lips close to Irma's cheek again.

"Oh, mother!" he whispered very low, "do not speak. Do you hear them? Those angels have come back again. They are singing now behind the tree."

And some say that it was true; but others say that it was only Gregor and his companions at the lower end of the hall, chanting their Christmas hymn:

All glory be to God on high,
And to the earth be peace!
Good-will, henceforth, from heaven to men
Begin, and never cease.

The First Christmas Tree

Henry Van Dyke